WELCOME

Collect the special coins in this book.
You will earn one gold coin for
every chapter you read.

Once you have finished all the chapters,
find out what to do with your gold coins at
the back of the book.

With special thanks to J.N. Richards

For Harry and Stanley Brown. Heroes in the making!

www.beastquest.co.uk

ORCHARD BOOKS

First published in Great Britain in 2018 by The Watts Publishing Group

1 3 5 7 9 10 8 6 4 2

Text © 2018 Beast Quest Limited.
Cover and inside illustrations by Steve Sims
© Beast Quest Limited 2018

Beast Quest is a registered trademark of Beast Quest Limited
Series created by Beast Quest Limited, London

A CIP catalogue record for this book is available from the British Library.

ISBN 978 1 40834 337 1

Printed in Great Britain

The paper and board used in this book are made from wood from responsible sources

Orchard Books
An imprint of Hachette Children's Group
Part of The Watts Publishing Group Limited
Carmelite House, 50 Victoria Embankment, London EC4Y 0DZ

An Hachette UK Company
www.hachette.co.uk
www.hachettechildrens.co.uk

Beast Quest®

LarnaK
THE SWARMING
MENACE

BY ADAM BLADE

ORCHARD

CONTENTS

Quake before me, Avantians. You think you are safe in your distant kingdom, but you couldn't be more wrong.

All of Makai is under my control. This island's ancient Beasts are risen again and obey my every word. The people are my slaves, building a force unlike any you've ever seen. I will do what my mother, Kensa, and my father, Sanpao, never could...I will have vengeance on Tom and his people.

You can muster your soldiers. You can assemble your navy. But you will never be ready.

I'll be seeing you very soon.

Your soon-to-be ruler,

Ria

THE MOUNTAIN PASS

"I won't last until nightfall." One-Eye let out a pained groan as the makeshift wagon trundled over the rocky mountain path.

From beside him on the raised seat of the mule-drawn cart, Tom saw Elenna roll her eyes. The pirate from Makai hadn't stopped complaining about the bumpiness of the road ever since they'd left Redsteel Forge.

Tom's hands tightened on the reins in his grasp, thinking that One-Eye could be a little bit more grateful. It was thanks to Tom and his friends that One-Eye had escaped at all. *So what if the ride is a little bumpy?* he thought. If the freed slaves of the forge had had their way, the pirate would have been executed on the spot. And Tom could hardly blame them – under Ria's harsh regime, they'd been beaten and starved as they toiled.

He gently flicked the mules' reins as he urged the animals along a tricky part of the trail. He wiped

away the sweat on his brow,
thinking of the Quest ahead. *If
that prisoner hadn't washed up
on Avantian shores, we'd never
have known about the four ancient*

Beasts Ria awoke, Tom thought. Now it was up to him and his friends to stop her from using those Beasts to invade Avantia.

The cart clattered over another big rock.

"Ouch!" One-Eye howled.

Daltec sighed from his position next to the former gangmaster. "I thought Makai pirates were the toughest around."

Elenna snorted with laughter.

Tom looked over his shoulder to see One-Eye scowling at the young wizard. "We don't all have magic to cushion ourselves," he mumbled.

Tom tutted. "Daltec would never waste his magic on making himself more comfortable. Not when there are far better uses for his powers."

"Like defeating Ria?" One-Eye questioned.

"Exactly," Daltec replied. "With Elenna's skill, Tom's bravery and my magic, Ria will be defeated."

"Yet somehow, my mistress got away." One-Eye was smirking. "And her plan to invade and conquer Avantia moves one step closer, while your so-called Quest appears to be failing."

Elenna whipped round in her seat. "Has the cart ride knocked the sense from your head?" she asked. "We defeated her Beast Menox the Sabre-Toothed Terror, halted her production of redsteel weapons, and freed the innocent people forced to work for her. Our Quest is going just fine."

One-Eye scoffed. "One Beast! Ria has others, and more clever plans than you could ever imagine."

"Just ignore him, Elenna," Tom said. "In this heat, we need to save our energy."

Elenna's jaw was still clenched, but she nodded and faced the path ahead.

Tom was grateful for his friend's determination. They would need it. Ria was young but she definitely took after her parents, Kensa and Sanpao, when it came to ruthlessness and scheming. She ran at the first sign of trouble, but knew how to make even worse trouble at every turn. He touched the blade-like tooth tucked into his belt, a token won for defeating Menox. *I've beaten Ria before; I'll do it again...*

As they reached the bottom of the mountain pass, dusk fell. The way ahead forked into two separate rocky paths and Tom realised that the mules would struggle to go much further. He pulled on the reins. "We'll travel the rest of the way on foot," he said.

"But which direction will you choose?" One-Eye asked. "I can lead you straight to Ria if you wish...for a price, of course."

Tom raised an eyebrow. One-Eye cast a pitiful figure with his bruises and scratches and the magical manacles that Daltec had conjured for his wrists. The pirate also seemed jumpy, his gaze darting to the left part of the fork and then back again.

"You're not exactly in a position to make deals," Tom pointed out. "You're our prisoner, and you'll be paid in our protection from any Beasts we meet." Tom and Elenna cut the mules loose. "Besides, I know which way Ria has gone. You keep on looking at the path on the left."

One-Eye glowered but said nothing. They walked on, soon

coming to another path that tracked along the base of the mountain before slanting upwards and passing through it.

"The way through the mountain is narrow," Daltec said, peering ahead.

"It's not supposed to be easy, is it, Avantian?" One-Eye scoffed. "That's the way of Makai. The roads here are treacherous to any who don't know them."

"Sounds about right," Elenna muttered. "An island made up of cutthroats with an equally cutthroat landscape."

They entered the narrow mountain passage, One-Eye leading the way.

"You know, in the good old days, these mountain paths were crawling with outlaws as fierce as lions." One-Eye's voice echoed off the sides of the walkway. "Bandits would stand as still and quiet as statues, wearing clothes that blended in with the rock face so they could ambush the unsuspecting." One-Eye suddenly stumbled and began to curse.

"Then I guess you can't be related to any of them," Elenna mused. "I mean, you're useless at staying quiet."

One-Eye stopped. "Perhaps I should stop leading the way if I'm so annoying," he huffed. "It's not very safe for me, you know? This path is going downhill and I can't hold on to anything for balance with these manacles."

"Keep walking." Elenna went to nudge the pirate forward along the path but Daltec stopped her.

"It does look treacherous ahead," the wizard said. "We should release him for this bit."

Tom nodded. "But we're watching you, One-Eye."

Daltec clicked his fingers and the manacles disintegrated in the air.

The pirate rubbed his wrists. "Most obliged. This way." One-Eye led them down the slope until they came to the edge of a gloomy, sunken canyon.

"We need to go down there?" Elenna asked.

One-Eye nodded. "There's a cave at the bottom that leads us out of the mountain altogether."

They trekked into the chasm, but halfway into the descent, One-Eye waved them over to a platform that jutted out over the canyon. "Look, you can see the cave properly from here."

"Good. I really can't wait to get out of this place." Elenna leant forward on the platform so she could have a proper look at the cave. "I miss the sky already."

"I couldn't agree more," Daltec said, joining her.

Goosebumps prickled on Tom's skin. "Are you sure this is the right way?" he asked the pirate. "This doesn't feel right."

"Of course it is," One-Eye said.

"The right way to death!"

Then he barrelled forward and shoved Tom and his two friends over the side of the platform.

INTO THE LIONS' DEN

Tom was too surprised even to scream as he tumbled through the gloominess of the sunken canyon. He reached out to grab at something, but his fingers just found air. There was no other way except down.

He hit the bottom of the pit, his knees buckling, and his body smashing to the ground. It hurt, but he was alive. He rolled on to all fours, searching for Elenna and Daltec. In the dim light he could see his friends staggering to their feet.

"Are you all right?"Tom asked, rushing to their side.

Elenna nodded. "Daltec managed to break our fall with some magic."

"It's a good thing, too," Daltec murmured, "or we'd be an even easier target."

"What do you mean?" Tom asked.

Daltec pointed at the cave that One-Eye had told them was the way out. Tom could see a pair of amber eyes glowing in the gloom. Tawny, furry bodies, thick with muscles,

padded towards them. Powerful-
looking jaws opened to reveal
glinting teeth.

Lions!

"Get behind me," Tom commanded,

lifting his shield, as the stalking lions began to encircle them. One of them was tracking their every move, and Tom guessed – from its thick, dark mane – that it was the pride leader.

Elenna went to nock an arrow, but stopped. "No use," she muttered. "I'll only be able to take down one."

The lion sprang towards her, but Tom was quicker. He leapt in front of his friend and threw up his shield. The lion's claws slammed into the wood, making Tom's whole arm shake.

Elenna and Daltec scrambled behind Tom, whilst the lion tore its claws from the shield and staggered backwards. It snarled as it examined its bloody nails.

Tom realised that the other lions had them completely encircled, but were not attacking. *They're waiting for the leader to draw blood first,* Tom thought. *But how long until they join the fight?*

He drew his sword. "Remember, these lions might not be our enemy, but we have to get out of this canyon alive. The whole of Avantia is depending on us."

With a snarl, the dark-maned lion attacked again and Tom struck out, whacking the creature with the flat of his blade.

The lion gave a pained snarl that

turned into a battle roar. Then all the
lions pounced as one. Tom knew that
neither his shield nor sword could
stop them.

The sound of roaring suddenly
shut off, and was replaced by a

low, thrumming noise. Tom looked about himself, seeing that he was surrounded by a force field that was almost completely translucent except for a hint of gold, humming with magical energy. The lions were

sprawled on the other side, snarling in confusion.

Turning to his left, Tom saw Daltec standing very still, his face tense, with sweat beading on his forehead as he kept his hands in the air.

"I'll hold the lions off for as long as I can," Daltec gasped. The force field shuddered as the lions tried to charge their way through and were thrown back.

Tom sheathed his sword, gazing around the canyon. The cave from which the lions had emerged was now completely empty. Inside it, he could see a narrow path.

"Follow me," Tom said and edged

forward, his friends right behind him. As they moved through the pride of lions, the animals swiped out with their claws, the magical barrier crackling from the blows.

Daltec's face was red, veins showing at his temples as he strained to keep the protective shield up.

"Not far now," Elenna shouted as they drew closer to the cave. "Then we can get away."

Just as long as there aren't any more lions hiding in the shadows, Tom thought to himself, his hand gripping the hilt of his sword.

They entered the cave and, as they did so, Daltec gave a rasping cry.

"I'm sorry," the wizard murmured.

"I can't… I can't—"

Daltec collapsed and Tom dived forward to catch him even as the force field disintegrated.

Tom could hear the padding footsteps of the lions behind them. *They're close!*

"Take Daltec," he told Elenna. "I'll hold off the lions and give you a head start."

Elenna hesitated. "All right, but be careful." She held up the sagging wizard as best she could and disappeared down the narrow path.

Tom turned to face the lions, deliberately standing at the neck of the winding path. He knew the constricted space meant the lions wouldn't be able to attack more than one at a time.

I'll have to take those odds.

He drew his sword, readying to battle the first lion, but a gasp from Elenna made him freeze.

"It's a dead end," she shouted. "One-Eye was lying when he said there was a way out of here."

Tom's grip tightened on the hilt of his sword. *Of course the pirate lied; just like he lied about everything else.* "Don't panic." He hoped his friend wouldn't hear the worry in his voice.

A lion leapt out of the darkness. Tom caught a glimpse of teeth and the glint claws and then he was knocked backwards. His head

slammed on to the ground and
he groaned, fragments of his
surroundings dancing in and out of
his vison, making him feel dizzy and
disorientated. The lion reared up
over him and raised its claws, ready
to slash down.

Tom called on the power of his
golden breastplate. It might have
been housed in the armoury at King
Hugo's palace in Avantia, but he
could still summon its magic when
he needed it. He felt strength surge
through him, clearing the dizzy
feeling. He kicked out at the lion.
Opening his eyes, he saw the animal
flying back, crashing into the pride
that waited at the mouth of the cave.

"Tom, there's a way through."
Elenna's voice sounded further away
than before. "It's really tight. The
lions won't be able to follow."

"You go. I'll be right behind
you." Tom followed the direction of

Elenna's voice, and the further he travelled along the path the lower the ceiling became, until he was crawling on his hands and knees. Up ahead he caught a glimpse of Daltec's cloak disappearing through a narrow hole. He dived after the wizard, but as he did so he heard the snap of teeth and felt something snag on his trailing leg. *My foot is in a lion's mouth!* Only the thick leather of his boot was protecting him. Tom tried to tug his foot free, feeling it slide all the way out of his boot.

He scrambled through the hole and emerged into the light on a mountain path.

Elenna grinned at him as she

helped him to his feet. "You took your time."

Tom pointed at his bootless foot. "Sorry, I had a bit of a close call."

"I can fix it." Daltec gave him a shaky smile. "Once I've had some rest. I'll conjure you a new boot."

Elenna looked worried. "We can't rest. One-Eye will be on his way to warn Ria. We need to try and stop him."

They climbed up to higher ground and Tom used the enhanced vision from his golden helmet to scour the terrain. There was no sign of Ria, nor a new Beast, but he could see One-Eye's footprints. The pirate didn't know it, but he was leading his enemies straight to his leader.

Further along the path, they heard the sound of buzzing and then a gust of fetid air rolled over them.

"What is that awful smell?" Elenna asked as they turned a corner on the track.

"It smells like death," Daltec murmured.

There, on the trail, was something large and rotting. Locusts buzzed all around it, like bees circling a flower. The sound they made was high-pitched and unrelenting. It made Tom's ears ache.

As they got closer, Tom realised that the carcass was actually the shed skin of some kind of creature.

"That casing belongs to something enormous," Elenna said, eyes wide.

Tom nodded. "A Beast, no doubt," he said. "And it's probably not far away."

THE ELIXIR WELLS

As the sun rose in the sky, Tom was pleased to see that Daltec's strength seemed to be coming back. The wizard led the way up a steep hill, and gasped as he reached the top. "I can't believe it," he breathed. "It really exists."

"What do you see?" Elenna asked, racing to the top of the hill also.

Tom followed, trying to ignore the pain of the rocky path slashing at his bare foot. Looking down, he saw a vast quarry, dug deep into an otherwise sprawling plain. Men in tatty, threadbare clothes swung heavy pickaxes at some fragments of rock. Sweat glinted on their skin in the fierce sunshine, and some were trying to find shelter beneath huge chunks of stone that floated in the air above them. Some were simply boulders, but others looked as large as the huts back in Tom's home village, Errinel. Complex ropes and pulleys and wobbly-looking wooden bridges connected the rocks with the ground, and miners scurried along

them like ants. The ground below
was spattered with what looked like
patches of violet mould.

"What are those things?" Tom asked, batting away a locust that buzzed around his head.

"Things as big as that shouldn't be able to float," Elenna said, waving another locust away. "It's unnatural."

"No…" Daltec murmured. "This is natural magic… These rocks are the Elixir Wells."

Elenna frowned as she stared at the hulking lumps of rock. "They don't look like any wells I've ever seen."

"Think of them more like vessels," Daltec said. "At their heart they contain Floating Elixir."

"The purple liquid that fuelled

Sanpao's flying ship!" Tom exclaimed, realising what the violet patches were. He remembered what the escaped slave at Hugo's palace had told them – Ria was planning to invade Avantia with an airborne fleet. It made sense that she'd need to stockpile the oil-like substance that made her ships defy gravity.

"Quick! Get down," Elenna cried, as several small flying dinghies controlled by pirates shot up from the ground. With his cheek pressed to the earth, Tom saw the pirates guide the dinghies right up to the Elixir Wells. He spotted Ria in one of the flying machines, standing next to a companion wearing a scarlet neckerchief. She was pointing at the rocks, and in the next moment a series of complex ropes and bridges were harnessed to the floating wells with huge bolts. The tired-looking miners on the ground scrambled up the ropes and began to trundle along the walkways.

"Faster," Ria barked, "or you'll be sorry."

The miners dipped their heads and raced along the high bridges before hacking at the floating rocks, releasing a thick, purple goo. Ria grinned in satisfaction as the dripping liquid formed an oozing, bubbling pool on the ground. At

the edges of the purple pond, more miners appeared. Using buckets and wearing thick gloves, they collected up the goo and transferred it into barrels, which floated off the ground as they were filled. The workers loaded them on to floating carts, tethering them in place.

Elenna lifted her head. "It was hard enough battling one pirate crew with a flying ship. A whole fleet, though..."

"We can't let that happen." Tom shifted into a crouching position. "We must stop this whole operation, and we must do it now. Follow me."

"You're not going anywhere, Tom," Daltec said. "Not without two boots on your feet." Daltec clicked his fingers and a small blue flame appeared at his fingertips. His face was strained as he tried to make the flame burn even brighter before he released it, and the fire twisted and turned itself around Tom's foot.

Tom could feel a tingling on his skin, the flame getting warmer and warmer until he worried that it might burn his skin; then the flame hardened and, in a flare of blue light, became a solid boot.

Tom grimaced as he looked at Daltec. "Is it me, or...is this a slightly different colour to my other boot?"

Elenna frowned, looking down at his feet. "It does look a bit...off."

Daltec scoffed. "I can fix the colour later, I…" Then he noticed that Tom and Elenna were grinning at him. "You're just joking, aren't you? Very funny!"

Tom clapped the wizard on the shoulder. "Thanks, Daltec."

Elenna put a hand on his shoulder. "We're not out of the woods yet. Look."

Down below, Ria had slotted a vial into one of the crevices of the wells. She then guided her dinghy a safe distance away, and nearby miners crouched down low on the rope bridges as the vial exploded and more purple liquid poured into the pool below, swiftly making it a lake.

Ria looked very pleased with herself as she floated towards another well. "This is our chance," Tom said.

Elenna nodded. "Whilst she's distracted trying to explode stuff, we can work out how to capture her."

"Daltec, can you make us invisible?" Tom asked.

"I'll try," the wizard replied. "But I confess, I'm not quite as well recovered as I thought."

"Stay here out of sight and do your best," Tom said.

Daltec's face was worried but he nodded, muttering a few words. Tom looked at Elenna, seeing her flicker in and out of sight. Gazing down at his own hand, he saw he was vanishing too.

Daltec's magic is working, but not perfectly, Tom thought as they crept down the path. *We need a proper hiding place – and quickly.*

Scanning the pit, he pointed over to a collection of empty barrels and he and Elenna ducked behind them.

Tom waited for a shout or a cry that would tell him that they had been spotted, but all he heard was the clank of pickaxes hitting rock.

Peeping from behind the barrel, Tom saw that Ria was almost directly above him, a rope trailing from her dinghy. In a few moments, he'd be able to leap up on to her craft using the power of his golden boots and take her by surprise.

He quickly explained the plan to Elenna.

"I'll cover you," she said, and drew an arrow from her quiver.

Tom bent his legs ready to leap up, but sensed someone staring at him. He looked up to see Ria glaring down. Daltec's magic had worn off.

"Intruders!" she roared, leaning over the side of her craft and hurling another vial.

The explosion was instant and the force of the blast threw Tom and Elenna in opposite directions.

"Elenna," Tom cried through the choking smoke. "Where are you?" Panic made his chest feel tight. He couldn't see his friend.

"You foolish Avantians." Ria's mocking voice echoed through the smog. "Did you really think you could ambush me?" She laughed nastily. "I can't be stopped."

"You're wrong," Tom shouted into the dust. "While there is blood in my veins, I'll—"

"Fail!" Ria interrupted. "You'll fail because I'm going to make sure this is your very last Quest."

The smoke was clearing and Tom saw that the miners had all scrambled out of the pit. Elenna was staggering to her feet. She looked dazed, but otherwise uninjured. Behind her, Tom saw the shadow of something emerge.

It was a giant locust-like Beast with six jointed legs and two pairs of wings that vibrated so fiercely they seemed to create sparks. Its

segmented body was covered with
a hard exoskeleton that had arrow-

like spines along its back. One of the spines was a bright gold, and seemed sharper than the others. Two eyes made up of hexagonal lenses protruded from its pointed head and Tom saw Elenna reflected in its fractured gaze.

The Beast opened its gaping jaws and sprang towards her.

LARNAK ATTACKS

Tom somersaulted through the air, landing with a thud in front of Elenna. She spun round to stand shoulder to shoulder with him, readying her bow. The Beast examined them balefully before a fierce chittering sound suddenly filled the air.

Thanks to the power of the red jewel in his belt, Tom could hear the Beast's shrill voice inside his head:

My name is Larnak. You don't belong here. You'll pay for your intrusion.

Tom quickly told Elenna what the Beast had said.

"Yup, I didn't think she was looking too friendly," Elenna replied with a sigh.

The Beast leapt forward, forcing them back.

"Whoa!" Elenna grabbed Tom's arm and pulled him towards her. "Watch your step."

Tom glanced over his shoulder and saw that he was right on the edge of the pool of purple elixir.

He gulped. He had no idea what

damage the elixir might cause if it touched his skin. *And I don't fancy finding out!*

Larnak's chittering became a high-pitched hum as she took flight, her wings becoming a blur. The noise made Tom want to tear off his own ears. The Beast hurtled in their direction like an arrow.

As he and Elenna threw themselves to the ground, Tom felt the gust from the Beast's wings roll over their heads. Larnak was doubling back in an arcing loop, before heading downwards once more. The Beast's strange jointed legs straightened and lengthened. Feet that glistened with an oozing substance stuck themselves to Tom and Elenna with a wet sucking sound.

Then they were airborne, the warm wind whipping at Tom's cheeks as the Beast took them higher and higher.

Elenna groped for an arrow, nocking it and firing at the Beast, only for the missile to bounce off Larnak's exoskeleton and hurtle back towards them, just missing their faces.

Elenna bit her lip. "The arrow was a bad idea."

"No, it wasn't," Tom said. "At least now we know this Beast has armour that can't be pierced."

"So how do we get out of this?" Elenna began to wriggle like fish bait on a line.

Tom studied the Beast's feet. He could see that the gluey substance it had produced there had hardened to form thick, scab-like crusts. *Scabs that need to be ripped away.*

"So nice of you to hang around like this," Ria's sneering voice said from behind them. "But take my advice and don't shoot yourself with your own arrows." Turning his head, Tom saw her hovering nearby in her small flying craft. "I'd much prefer to kill you myself."

"Keep dreaming," Elenna growled, and pulled back her bowstring to fire two arrows into the hull of Ria's flying vessel.

Ria screeched with fury as her dinghy began to leak purple elixir and dipped suddenly. She gripped the sides for balance.

"Quick, Elenna, grab a rope," Tom

said, as an idea came to him. They grasped the nearest trailing ropes. As Ria's ship plummeted downwards, the thick crusts that held them were ripped away, and they were freed from the Beast's grip.

The dinghy hurtled to the ground and, just as it looked like it was about to crash, Tom released his rope and somersaulted through the air, landing on the balls of his feet. Elenna landed just as gracefully beside him.

With the extra weight gone, Ria's dinghy shot back upwards and she finally managed to get it under control while her assistant swiftly patched up the damage caused by

Elenna's arrows.

Larnak was just a dot in the sky and Tom wondered if they had actually managed to injure her.

"Think you can get away that easily?" Ria cried. She pointed at several of her pirates, who lined the lip of the pit. "Kill them!"

Ria's men poured into the quarry, some wielding cutlasses, others sharp tools that they had snatched from miners.

Tom and Elenna stood back to back, ready to fight; but before the pirates reached them, the air began to crackle with energy, and a glowing magical net fell from the sky, trapping Ria's men in a writhing bundle of limbs.

Tom looked up to where Daltec stood on the hilltop. The wizard's face was determined but strained, and Tom knew that the net might not hold for long.

A familiar chittering noise filled

the air, and a moment later, Larnak appeared again, hovering over the quarry. Miners along the perimeter of the pit dropped to their knees and covered their heads. Those who had stayed in the mine dived behind barrels and piles of rock.

The wails of fear from both pirates and miners and the sound seemed to draw Larnak like a moth to a flame. She landed on the ground and began to stalk towards a cluster of barrels where two miners were hiding.

"Oh no," Elenna said. "They won't stand a chance."

"It's all right," Tom said. "I have an idea."

He ran towards the Beast, waving

his sword above his head, touching his red jewel so Larnak could hear him: "Going for the easy prey?" he taunted. "Are you scared to fight a Master of the Beasts?"

The Beast swung away from the miners and turned to face Tom instead, her voice a screech in Tom's mind. *Scared?*

Tom walked backwards, knowing there was a pile of rocks directly behind him. *Time to put this plan into action*, he thought, and pretended to stumble, falling to his knees with a cry.

Larnak gave a shriek of triumph and charged at Tom. As the shadow of the Beast covered him, Tom used the power of his golden boots to leap upwards. As he somersaulted through the air, he watched Larnak charge headfirst towards the pile of rocks.

Yes, he thought. But instead of the Beast's exoskeleton being shattered

by the rocks, Larnak's body simply exploded like a wave hitting the shoreline, shattering into a swarm of hundreds of small locusts that rose, buzzing, into the air...

...and then flew straight towards him.

THE SWARM ASCENDS

The locusts covered Tom completely, the swarm so dense that it left him completely blind. They slammed into his body on every side, pulling at his hair and clothes, their wings scratching at his face and eyes. He flailed wildly, and helplessly, unable to get clear of them. Then, suddenly, he felt weightless.

The swarm was lifting him off the ground!

Through a tiny, shifting gap he saw that other swarms had seized his friends too, and were lifting them skyward.

"Tom! Daltec!" Elenna cried, her voice filled with panic. "Are you safe?

"I'm all right, but my magic is exhausted." Daltec's voice was almost drowned out by the hum of hundreds of locusts.

"I'm fine as well, Elenna," Tom shouted.

"Not for long!" Ria cackled and Tom caught a glimpse of her through the swarming locusts, standing in

her airborne dinghy and pointing. "Dump them over there." Tom looked where she was pointing, and saw one of the floating elixir wells was nearby.

The swarm obeyed, carrying Tom until he was directly over one of the wells, then letting him go. He fell for a moment, landing with a thud on one of the hovering lumps of rock. Elenna and Daltec were dropped beside him.

Elenna scrambled to her feet, flicking angrily at a few locusts that still buzzed nearby. "I really hate insects." She looked around her. "Especially ones that do a pirate's bidding. What do you think Ria has planned for us?"

Daltec frowned, pointing to the ground. "I'll bet he has a good idea." Tom looked down, seeing One-Eye leering up at them.

"Nice to see you again," the pirate shouted. He was weighing something up in his hand. "I've got a gift for you." When the pirate drew back his arm, Tom saw a glass vial filled with red liquid.

Then One-Eye threw it at their floating well. The vial exploded on the rock, the well dipping violently to one side. Tom was thrown forward, but swiftly wedged his sword in the rock's crevice to steady himself. He saw Elenna kneel and keep low

as the rock continued to tilt from
side to side, but Daltec had lost his
balance and was sliding backwards
towards the edge – and a deadly
drop to the ground.

Elenna dived towards the wizard

and just managed to grab one of his boots. Straining forward, Tom caught Elenna's foot and used the strength from his golden breastplate to drag both of his friends back to the middle of the floating rock.

"Thank you," Daltec gasped.

"You have nothing to thank us for," Tom replied as the rock continued to tilt in the sky. He noticed that the explosion had made a small hole in the well and purple elixir dripped from it. They were also completely surrounded by pirates in dinghies who were gleefully brandishing weapons. *Sitting ducks...*

"Tom's right. We're on this Quest

together and—"Elenna broke off and ducked as a pickaxe spun straight towards her.

The pirates in the dinghies roared with disappointment as the pickaxe missed its target and they began hurling yet more weapons. Tom yanked his sword from the stone, ready to cut down the flying missiles, but Daltec was quicker and jumped in front of Tom. A shower of sparks left his fingertips and blasted the oncoming weapons into pieces.

Elenna let out a breath. "Like I was saying, we watch each other's backs."

Tom tried to respond, but his voice was drowned out by a deafening humming sound. Looking up, he saw that Larnak had reformed herself and was watching them with shiny, dark eyes.

Tom held his sword high and the Beast slowly descended on buzzing wings until she loomed directly above them. There was a clicking sound and the arrowed spines along Larnak's back vibrated violently.

The Beast gave a roar of fury. Her mandibles spread wide and a jet of thick gunge shot out of her mouth. With nowhere to run, Tom raised his hands as the goo spattered over him.

As he tried to wipe the foul substance away, his arms began to feel heavy. It was hard even to move.

It's solidifying!

"I'm stuck," Daltec cried. "I can't move my feet. I can't move anything!"

Tom turned his neck, but even that was hard. His friends were

covered too, twisting and writhing
as the gunge set across their bodies.

"Larnak's trapped us in some kind
of cocoon," Elenna exclaimed.

Tom searched for something that
might help them, even as the gloop

hardened around his neck and chest like mortar.

There's nothing here, Tom realised. *Nothing here except rocks, and the purple elixir.*

Tom could feel the gluey substance trickling down his face. Soon it would reach his eyes, his nose, his mouth…and there would be nothing he could do.

Ria floated into view and smiled at them. "If you're lucky, you're going to be suffocated," she sneered. "And if you're unlucky, Larnak will have you for dinner first." She shrugged. "Though why a Beast would want to eat something as unpalatable and pathetic as you three, I don't know.

Come on, the rest of you. We have work to do."

She turned her dinghy and zipped away, and the rest of the pirates followed.

Ria's disappearing boat was the last thing Tom saw as the sticky goo covered his eyes and he was plunged into darkness.

6

COFFINS

Tom could hardly breathe in his insect coffin. He wanted to scream, but his chest was bound too tightly.

I need to calm down, Tom told himself. He wanted desperately to breathe, but he couldn't open his lips at all. He tried to focus, to harness the magical strength from his golden breastplate, which had saved him on so many Quests in the past.

Help me, he willed. *One more time.*

Power began to radiate through his arms, and he pushed out against the hardness of his cocoon. The last of his breath ran out in his lungs, replaced with a slow, terrible burn. *Come on!* The second skin of the dried resin wasn't giving at all. *This is it*, Tom realised. *I'm not getting out of this Quest alive.* He felt himself slipping into unconsciousness...

No! Concentrate! He fought the tide of blackness threatening to overwhelm him, clenching his fists

and feeling his strength gather.
Something cracked around his
knuckles, and hope flooded through
his heart.

It's working!

He managed to shift his arm,
and felt the kiss of cool air on his
skin. A piece of cocoon had broken
and fallen off! With a grunt, he
wrenched his arm free completely
and reached up to tear off his
cocoon mask. It came away in a
chunk and he gulped in a lungful of
air. Relishing the freedom, he tore
away at his prison.

He spun round to see that Elenna
and Daltec were both still entombed
within their cocoons. Standing

between his trapped friends, he began clawing at the two hard shells, starting with their heads. As he worked, he glanced up to check neither Ria nor any of her men were watching them. They were far too busy throwing explosives at the different Elixir Wells. Larnak's hum was close, but Tom could not see her, so he continued tearing at the cocoons, ignoring the pain in his fingers. As soon as Elenna's face was clear, she gave a spluttering cough, and Daltec's mouth opened to gulp in a desperate breath. Tom sighed in relief, and soon they were breaking free with their own hands.

Elenna's eyes were wide. "I really thought that was it." She shook her

head. "When it all went dark, I
thought we'd failed. That Ria had
defeated us."

Daltec's face was pained. "I'm sorry that I had no magic to save you. What kind of wizard am I?"

"One who has protected us countless times," Tom told him. "We might not have your magic, but there are other ways to defeat Ria and Larnak. We just need to find them."

Tom watched the dinghies that floated in the air nearby. The pirates were still busy with their explosives and they didn't seem that concerned about the big chunks of rock that hurtled to ground below, almost flattening the miners. To their left, he spotted Larnak hovering lazily in the air. She was making sure that none of her slaves tried to escape the pit.

"We have to get airborne," Tom said to his friends. "Then we can battle Larnak properly and finish her once and for all."

"Then we'll deal with Ria," Daltec said.

Elenna nodded. "So we need one of those dinghies!"

Daltec rubbed his hands together and a few sparks appeared. "I think I can help, but you need to give me a moment."

Tom leant forward and dipped his shield in some of the purple elixir that oozed from their well. He released it and grinned as he saw that the shield floated, just as he'd hoped. *Perfect.*

"You get the dinghy. I'll distract Larnak and the pirates."

"We won't be long," Elenna promised.

Tom stared at the shield. *I really hope this works!* He backed up as far as he could and then, calling on the power of his golden leg armour, sprinted forward. He jumped off the side of the rock on to the shield, arms spread for balance. Then he was hurtling across the sky. Several pirates saw him coming, and brandished their weapons in cries of alarm. Tom tilted his body to steer a path between them. The villains hurled weapons at Tom, but he was too fast. Weaving from side to side, he dodged a pickaxe and then a shovel and a cutlass, which grazed the top of his head.

Close one!

"Larnak!" Ria bellowed, as she turned her own craft towards him. "Stop that wretch!"

Tom shot towards her, drawing his sword, but suddenly the humming was deafening.

Larnak's massive form appeared, blocking his path.

1

EXPLODING SKY

Larnak struck out with one of her powerful jointed legs, but Tom dodged it and darted away from her. Down below, Daltec conjured a magical lasso, which he looped around one of the flying dinghies. Tom knew the pirates inside were unarmed – they had thrown all their weapons at him! As Elenna withdrew an arrow from her quiver, the pirates leapt out of the dinghy, on to one of the rope bridges below.

Tom smiled. The plan was working even better than he'd hoped. He turned to face Ria, who was just a few arm-lengths away now. He pointed his sword at the pirate. "It's over!"

"Never!" Ria shouted back. She nodded at the Beast. "Kill him!"

Larnak's body quivered in anticipation, the golden, sharpest spine glinting in the fierce sunlight. She charged at Tom, and he raced to meet her head-on, bringing his sword across her hard flank, creating a

shower of sparks.

Larnak turned her head, opening her mandibles and firing a jet of foul-smelling gunk at Tom. He ducked, hearing the substance smack into Ria's dinghy. He turned to see the vessel spinning through the sky as she fought with the tiller to control it. At the last moment, she leapt off, landing in a craft below, piloted by One-Eye. Her out-of-control dinghy crashed into one of the floating wells.

Tom covered his eyes as the dinghy exploded in a blaze of purple light. Daring to look again, he spotted Larnak hurtling upwards away from the explosion. As the blast faded, Tom saw that the well was bleeding elixir. As it did, the huge rock began to sink through the air.

Ria was steering her dinghy down towards the ground, where the leaking purple fuel was pooling.

"Gather it up into barrels!' she shouted at the pirates and workers around the pit. "It mustn't go to waste."

"But what about him?" asked One-Eye, pointing up at Tom.

Ria's eyes glinted and she shoved One-Eye out of the boat. He landed with a thump on the ground. "You and Larnak can deal with one little boy, can't you?"

With that, she took off again, flying away from the wells at speed.

Elenna and Daltec steered their floating dinghy over to where Tom hovered on his board. Elenna's expression was grim as her gaze followed the vessel that was zooming away. "We'll chase her down!"

Tom shook his head. "It's more important that we destroy the elixir. That way, Ria won't ever be able to use it to attack Avantia."

Daltec pointed at his feet. "We have just the thing."

Tom drifted closer and saw that the dinghy was filled with earthenware pots of grubby glass

vials like the ones the pirates and
Ria had been throwing.

"Good thinking," said Tom. "Let's
rig all the wells and barrels with
explosives."

With a huge boom below, the
drained rock hit the ground with
a mighty crash, scattering workers
and throwing up curtains of purple
spray. As the commotion died down,
Tom heard a familiar humming
noise.

The Beast is close.

Tom kicked off on his shield,
and from above he could hear
Larnak's strange chittering sound.
He raced upwards to confront the
Beast. Larnak lashed out with her

tail, hitting Tom in the chest and knocking him off his shield. Tom toppled to one side but managed to grab the edge of his shield before he fell to his death. His chest felt like it was on fire from the blow, but

he held on and guided the shield
upwards so that he was directly
above Larnak.

There it is. Tom stared at the
arrowed spine that looked different
from the others. It shone and
glimmered with magic. *Maybe
destroying this spine is the key to
destroying the Beast.* He jumped on
his shield once more and sped on
the air towards his foe.

Then he lurched and plunged, as
if an invisible hand was pulling
him to the ground. Looking down,
past his boots, Tom realised that
the shield had almost lost all of its
elixir. Leaning forward, he swung
his sword at the Beast's golden

spine, but it bounced off harmlessly.

Larnak gave a roar of pain and, in an instant, Tom found himself surrounded once again by hundreds of locusts. He fell through the swarm of hard bodies, wings and legs scratching his cheeks – and then the locusts were gone once more, and Tom was in the painful grasp of the Beast's mandibles. *She can burst apart and re-form whenever she wants! How can I defeat a Beast who isn't even there?*

He thrashed as hard as he could, but the mandibles just gripped him tighter and tighter until he thought his ribs might shatter. He wedged his shield under one mandible and struck out with his sword at the other. The mandible loosened for just a second, only for Larnak to tighten her grip. Tom growled in frustration, looking down as he desperately tried to think of another way out...

That was when he spotted Elenna and Daltec racing away from the floating wells. They were gesturing to Tom that he should cover his head.

The wells are going to blow, Tom realised, crouching on his shield and bracing himself.

BOOM!

The shockwaves sent the Beast flying backwards, and she released

Tom from her grip. He found himself spinning through the air, desperately clinging to his shield. Though the chaos of rock fragments and dust, he saw locusts swarming in confusion before they flooded together once more in the shape of the Beast.

This is my chance to get the golden spine, Tom realised. He tried to guide his shield towards the Beast's back, but Larnak's wings were vibrating even faster than before. A downdraught drove him beneath the Beasts, where he could see that her underbelly was bare of any armour. *I've got a new idea...*

Tom struck out with his sword, but as his blade connected, the Beast morphed into a swarm again. His momentum made him overbalance, and his feet left his shield.

And there was nothing to stop Tom's fall.

RAINING ROCK

Tom flailed as he toppled, hoping to grab his shield and call on Arcta's feather to slow his descent. But he missed and plummeted. *This is it!* he thought, hoping his death would be quick…

Splash!

It took a moment of panic and confusion to realise he'd landed in the elixir lake. Covered from head to toe in the purple liquid, he tried to crawl free but instead found himself floating up from the lake, as if a giant hand had picked him up and was guiding his every movement.

I'm completely weightless!

A moment later his shield landed in the liquid as well, then began to float. He snatched it from mid-air.

There was a thud to his left. Tom turned and saw that Larnak had re-formed and landed on the bank of the lake, watching him with greedy eyes and an open mouth as he hovered helplessly. And worse still, a gentle breeze was blowing him slowly towards her gnashing mandibles.

Tom felt a ball of dread form in his gut. *While I'm covered in this stuff, I don't stand a chance. But most of the elixir is on my clothes, so I wonder…*

Swiftly, Tom pulled off his tunic and breeches, until he was just in his underclothes. As he had hoped would happen, he began to sink, and his bare feet touched the ground.

Above, Tom watched his clothes float away. He felt more like a morsel of food than ever.

I've never had to face a Beast half-naked before…

Larnak stalked towards him,

rocks crunching beneath her feet.
Tom raised his sword, but the metal
was still coated in the purple fuel
and tried to lift him into the air.

Looking up, he saw Elenna and Daltec rigging another floating well with explosives. Elenna stopped as she spotted Tom. She looked unsure whether to continue.

Tom nodded. Just then, an idea popped into his head. *Perhaps there is another way to stop this Beast.* Elenna nodded back. Dropping his sword, Tom raced across the quarry. He could hear the chittering of Larnak right behind him, and he quickened his pace so that he stopped directly beneath the well that Elenna and Daltec had rigged.

He dropped down and covered his ears as the well above him exploded with another, louder *BOOM!*

Purple elixir was pouring on to the ground just next to Tom, landing in great spattering globules and splashing his body. Larnak was shaking her head. The explosion had disorientated her, but she seemed to regain herself and staggered towards him.

Do not move, Tom told himself as the Beast drew closer. *Not yet... Not until you hear the rocks fall.*

There was a creaking sound, and then a low whistling as the well above began to drop. The Beast's buggy eyes were fixed on Tom. *She thinks she's got me where she wants me...*

She closed in. Twenty paces, ten, five. Her mandibles drooled in

anticipation of her feast. Tom saw the shadow of the well fall over her.

"Got you!" he cried, then dived away. As he did, the giant rock landed on top of Larnak.

The Beast gave a desperate, angry shriek that was cut short as she was pinned to the ground. A few stray locusts broke free and flew away. But the rest were simply buried under the weight of rock. All that remained was the single spine, a token left behind by the vanquished Beast.

Elenna and Daltec managed to recover Tom's clothes, and luckily the young wizard knew a laundry spell. Tom pulled his tunic back on, and then his boots. All the pirates had run off when they saw Larnak defeated, so the only people left were the workers, freed from their enslavement. Tom had told them to return to their homes, but most had remained for one final task. Picking up their picks and shovels, and using carts and barrows, they'd emptied rocks into the elixir pool, filling it in completely until not a trace remained.

"This precious elixir will always be a part of Makai," said Daltc, "but if anyone wants to get hold of it, it'll be very hard work."

Tom saw that Elenna was frowning.

"What's the matter?" he asked.

"I was speaking to one of the miners," she said. "He said that Ria had already taken away hundreds of barrels."

"Enough to power an entire fleet," said Tom, reading her thoughts.

"Which means our Quest is still absolutely vital," Daltec murmured. One flying dinghy remained, and the three friends climbed into it. Waving farewell to the miners, they rose away from the remains of the wells in the direction the pirates had fled, until they crested a ridge.

Where've you fled to now, Ria?

Tom wondered.

Staring out into the distance, he
saw a vast jungle. From the looks of
it, a huge swathe had already been
cut down.

"That's where she'll be," he said.

"What makes you say that?" asked Daltec.

"She's building a fleet, isn't she? That means she'll need timber."

Tom turned the dinghy's tiller to set a course, narrowing his eyes. *While there's blood in my veins, that evil witch will never leave these shores...*

THE END

CONGRATULATIONS, YOU HAVE COMPLETED THIS QUEST!

At the end of each chapter you were awarded a special gold coin.
The QUEST in this book was worth an amazing 8 coins.

Look at the Beast Quest totem picture inside the back cover of this book to see how far you've come in your journey to become

MASTER OF THE BEASTS.

The more books you read, the more coins you will collect!

Do you want your own
Beast Quest Totem?

1. Cut out and collect the coin below
2. Go to the Beast Quest website
3. Download and print out your totem
4. Add your coin to the totem
www.beastquest.co.uk/totem

Don't miss the next exciting Beast Quest book, JUROG, HAMMER OF THE JUNGLE!

Read on for a sneak peek...

TROPICAL STORM

Tom's stomach lurched as the flying dinghy listed sharply with a sudden updraft, pitching him against its wooden rail. In a jumble of limbs, Elenna slid down the bench and slammed into his side. The forested hills of Makai swam sickeningly far below. *If we tip any further we're going to capsize!*

"Lean right!" he told Elenna. She grabbed the rail on her side of the boat. Tom braced his muscles and shifted his weight towards her. The boat levelled and he let out a breath of relief.

"Flying's...even...worse...than sailing..." Daltec panted, his face greyish green as he frowned back at them from his seat at the bow.

"It's this boat!" Tom grunted, both hands on the wooden tiller, trying to hold it steady. "I don't think it was meant for strong winds, only for short flights."

Tom, Elenna and Daltec had taken the flying boat from the Elixir Wells, where their pirate enemy Ria had been mining the floating fuel to power her flying ships. As well as defeating Larnak the Swarming Menace, Tom and his friends had managed to drain away much of the elixir in the wells before escaping. Unfortunately, Tom suspected that Ria had already mined enough to launch an attack on Avantia from the sky. Their only hope now was to stop Ria building her magical ships. *But somehow, we'll have to find her first...*

"We're heading for a storm," Elenna said, pointing. Ahead, the scattered clouds of Makai drew together, casting deep shadows over the jungle below. Even as Tom watched, the dark clouds thickened and swelled, rolling across the sky.

Tom clenched his teeth. "Just what we need!" He closed his eyes to summon the strength from his golden breastplate, which was part of his Golden Armour. The suit stood on display back in King Hugo's palace, but Tom could call on its magic wherever he was. He heaved at the tiller, trying to steer the dinghy around the angry-looking bank of cloud. But at the same moment, a strong wind slammed into the keel, making the craft judder. The sunlight

darkened to a murky brown and a
curtain of rain spread down from
the clouds ahead. Forked lightning
crackled across the sky, followed by
a rumble of thunder.

Suddenly, the boat pitched. Tom clung to the gunwale with one hand to stop himself falling against Elenna. Daltec whimpered.

The gloom deepened. A rush of heavy rain hit Tom's face. He braced his arms, using every muscle to keep the tiller steady, but mighty gusts tore at his body, straining his grip, driving the boat ever closer to the heart of the storm.

"Hold on!" Tom cried as the boat tipped suddenly forwards, making his stomach drop away. Another gust righted the dinghy, slamming Tom back on to the bench. Elenna crashed down, half on top of him, then slid back into her seat. Rain pelted them from every direction.

"Aargh!" The tiny dinghy rolled hard to the right, tearing his hand from the tiller. The craft began to spin, faster by the moment, whirling like water down a drain.

"Brace yourselves!" Tom called. "We're going to crash!" He crouched low, hugging the deck. At his side Elenna did the same.

Pop! Silence rang in Tom's ears as the buffeting wind and driving rain stopped. *No...* Tom could still see the rain lashing down as they spun, but somehow it didn't reach them. A faint blueish glow surrounded their boat. At the bow, Daltec now sat upright, chanting under his

breath. *He's created a forcefield!*
The wizard's body trembled and the
sinews stood out on his arms with
the effort of working his spell.

"He won't be able to hold the
forcefield for long!" Elenna said.

Tom heaved at the tiller, finally
managing to bring the boat out of its
downwards spin. *Crack!* A sizzling
flash of white exploded in his vision.
Daltec let out a cry, and the glowing
bubble surrounding their boat
flickered. Then it popped, sending a
shower of fizzing sparks cascading
downwards.

All at once the rain and wind hit
with full force. A forked tongue of
lightning hit the keel. *No!* Tom's

chest tightened with horror as he
saw purple elixir flowing from a
hole burned in the wood, leaving
a glittering trail behind them. His
stomach leapt into his mouth as

they plummeted, losing height fast, the boat's prow angled downwards, cutting through the storm towards the ground.

Tom threw up his shield, calling on the power of Arcta's eagle feather to slow their fall. He felt himself lift from his seat and grabbed the slick wood of the bench with his free hand. The weight of the boat almost tore Tom's arms from their sockets. Using the magical strength of his breastplate he braced his arms between his shield and the boat… But still they sped towards the treetops below.

"The boat's too heavy – we'll have to jump!" Tom cried.

"No! We'll break our legs, or worse!" Daltec shouted.

"I can heal broken bones," Tom said. "But I can't bring us back to life. Jump! Now!"

"No!" Daltec cried. "I've got a better plan." Tom saw his friend wave one hand, tracing a bright rune in the air, then flick his fingers towards the ground, sending a stream of fizzing blue energy bolts down through the tree canopy. "Hold on tight!" Daltec cried.

Read

JUROG, HAMMER OF THE JUNGLE

to find out what happens next!

Fight the Beasts,
Fear the Magic

Do you want to know more
about BEAST QUEST?
Then join our Quest Club!

Visit
www.beastquest.co.uk/club
and sign up today!

Are you a collector of the Beast Quest Cards?
Visit the website for further information.

OUT NOW!

The epic adventure is brought
to life on **Xbox One** and **PS4**
for the first time ever!

www.maximumgames.com   www.beast-quest.com

TEAMHEROBOOKS.CO.UK
DARE TO BE DIFFERENT